A QUILTER'S WISDOM

A QUILTER'S WISDOM

Conversations with Aunt Jane

BASED ON A HISTORIC TEXT BY
ELIZA CALVERT HALL

Illustrations by Anna Price-Oneglia
Introduction by Roderick Kiracofe

CHRONICLE BOOKS
SAN FRANCISCO

The text that appears in *A Quilter's Wisdom: Conversations with Aunt Jane* is based on a chapter from *Aunt Jane of Kentucky* by Eliza Calvert Hall, originally published in 1907. It has been edited by Allen D. Bragdon and adapted by Chronicle Books for publication in this form.

Printed in Hong Kong.

Library of Congress Cataloging-in-Publication Data available.

ISBN: 0-8118-0333-3

Distributed in Canada by Raincoast Books
112 East Third Avenue
Vancouver, B.C. V5T 1C8

10 9 8 7 6 5 4 3 2 1

Chronicle Books
275 Fifth Street
San Francisco, CA 94103

A Quilter's Wisdom

To my way of thinking, Aunt Jane of Kentucky is an ideal personification of the American quiltmaker. The invention of writer Eliza Calvert Hall, Aunt Jane came to seem a real person after her introduction to the public in Hall's 1907 bestseller, *Aunt Jane of Kentucky*.

In that collection of short stories, Aunt Jane Parrish was presented as a self-reliant widow, living happily with her memories and quilts in rural Kentucky. An unnamed niece coaxed stories out of the elderly lady who told of quiltmaking and of caring for them, of county fairs, family histories, unhappy marriages, women triumphing over adversity (usually shiftless men), church politics, horse races, and her enduring love for her kind and upright husband, Abram.

Aunt Jane of Kentucky went through more than twenty-three editions, and Aunt Jane emerged as a national folk heroine, quoted and praised, like Uncle Sam, Casey Jones, Betsy Ross, and John Henry. The line between fiction and nonfiction blurred beyond retrieval, but like her folksy counterparts, Aunt Jane spoke directly to the American heart.

Aunt Jane has been out of print for decades but she is still referred to in quilt books, both historical and how-to. Her musings about the nature of quiltmaking have been quoted and requoted, authors sometimes pointing out Aunt Jane as a fictional character, sometimes not.

Aunt Jane's clear sense of herself as a self-sufficient, autonomous person particularly appealed to Hall's readers.

In her time, the American belief in the primacy and power of the individual was unquestioned, and it was an attitude being earnestly appropriated by women.

"Did you ever think, child, how much piecin' a quilt's like livin' a life?" Aunt Jane asks her niece. Then she explains in plain, heartfelt language about picking out calico, "caliker," and patterns. A firm believer in free will, Aunt Jane makes a case that every person is in charge of her own life, whatever fate the Lord provides. "The Lord sends us the pieces," Aunt Jane goes on, "but we can cut 'em out and put 'em together pretty much to suit ourselves, and there's a heap more in the cuttin' out and the sewin' than there is in the caliker."

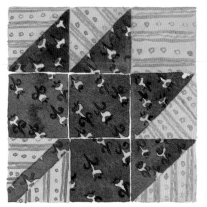

Palm Leaf

Though quilts first arrived in North America with

the English settlers, thousands of American women refined the craft of quiltmaking. Scholarship over the last two decades has unearthed many of the names and stories of these women, but most quiltmakers are anonymous, their lives lost in the haze of the past. This is one of the reasons I am so fond of Aunt Jane. She is a superb fictional representation of those lost women and lost stories. A cheerful, hardworking woman brimming with common sense and self-confidence, she is a very good stand-in for all the forgotten Aunt Janes, whose lives are known to us today only through their magnificent, unsigned quilts.

Besides the character herself, *Aunt Jane of Kentucky* is a fascinating window on the world of the quilter, the lore of quiltmaking, and the quilt revival. Quilts have been periodically rediscovered by the popular culture in the United States, but quilts have never been close to fading out of our national experience. The 1876 Centennial of the American Revolution sparked a high interest in colonial history and culture, such interest periodically bubbled to the surface while American women continued, as they had for two hundred years, making their beloved quilts. In the 1890s and early 1900s many articles in the influential women's magazines reflected a new surge of attention, the *Ladies Home Journal* in particular emphasizing the "rediscovery" of an American art form.

By having Aunt Jane speak to her modern young kinswoman, Hall's stories emphasized the historic aspect of quiltmaking, giving quilts a mystique and romance. Aunt Jane's oral histories of quilts are the kind of comforting stories that have been handed down among Americans for generations, some true and some not. It is important, however, to know these stories because sometimes what we want to believe tells us more about ourselves than the facts.

It is easy to read between Aunt Jane's lines and see quilts for what they were to women: a much-needed creative outlet and a means of socializing and bonding.

Aunt Jane, who would have made a good politician, chastises those (presumably men) who denigrate quilting as "a waste o' time" but is equally disapproving of women neglecting their other duties for the joys of quilting, providing one of her sweetest anecdotes about the hapless quilter Sarah Jane and her indulgent husband, Sam.

Pine Burr Quilt

In her strict ideas about duty and hard work, Aunt Jane is an accurate reflection of the late nineteenth- and early twentieth-century work ethic. She loves her quilts but

Peek-a-Boo Quilt

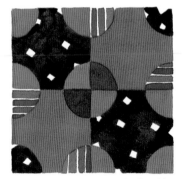

Mill Wheel Quilt

believes that too much passion is a dangerous thing, thus her quiltwork is carefully relegated to its place in the scheme of things. Yet Aunt Jane's passion for her quilts can't be completely hidden and also illuminates the competitiveness that was a sub-rosa element among quiltmakers. The elderly lady is perhaps as proud of prizes as of the quilts. The most compelling testimony to Aunt Jane's rectitude and discipline is revealed in her generous act of hiding her own perfect quilt so poor Sarah Jane can finally win a prize.

Perhaps Aunt Jane's chief appeal for me as a student of quilts is her keen awareness of the fabrics that make up a quilt. She loves to talk about the provenance of the fabric even more than the patterns or her own handiwork. "Some folks has albums to put folks' pictures in to remember 'em by, and some folks has a book and writes down the things that happen every day so they won't forgit 'em," says Aunt Jane to her niece. "Honey, these quilts is my albums and my di'ries. . . . There ain't nothin' like a piece o' caliker for bringing back old times. . . ."

The old times of Aunt Jane probably did not exist, for anyone, in the sentimental, goodness-triumphant version that Eliza Calvert Hall has shaped them in, but they are cheering, honest tales that make a bracing antidote to our own trying and often pessimistic stories. Like most writers who thrive on topicality, Hall's popularity has not lasted. Yet her talent for recasting the concerns of her day into accessible, vividly written stories is impressive. A suffragist and champion of women's issues, Hall's first big success was a short story called "Sally Ann's Experience." Aunt Jane made her first appearance in the story, which was published in *Cosmopolitan* magazine in 1898.

"Sally Ann's Experience" was republished a number of times and finally incorporated into Hall's first book, *Aunt Jane of Kentucky,* a collection of short stories narrated by Aunt Jane and peopled with her family, friends, and neighbors of Warren County, Kentucky. Aunt Jane was rejected by eight New York publishers before finally getting into print. Hall was repeatedly told dialect would never sell. (Indeed, the dialect has

Lady of the Lake

been softened in the story excerpted here.) The book was an immediate hit and reissued until the 1930s. A special fifty-cent edition alone sold more than 75,000 copies.

The woman behind Aunt Jane was as impressive as her character. Born Eliza Caroline Hall in Bowling Green, Kentucky, in 1856, she was the daughter of Dr. Thomas Chalmers Hall and Margaret Younglove Calvert Hall. Eliza Hall attended Western College in Oxford, Ohio, for one year. In 1885 she married a former Confederate officer, Major William Alexander Obenchain, a mathematics professor (and later president) of Ogden College in Bowling Green.

Writing under the name of Eliza Calvert Hall, most likely to honor her mother, Hall published poetry in *Scribner's Magazine*, wrote a variety of articles for the *New York Times, Harper's* magazine, *Century* magazine, and

Munsey's and also contributed to women's rights publications such as the *Women's Journal of Boston.* Under the name Mrs. Lida Calvert Obenchain she published women's rights pamphlets.

Hall, who had four children and lived in Dallas in her later life, was a president of the Equal Rights Association of Kentucky. She was also very interested in the mountain schools of Kentucky. Propelled by the arts-and-crafts movement and the revival of interest in American handiwork and traditions, these institutions sprang up throughout America in the late nineteenth and early twentieth century. They were founded not only to perpetuate local arts and crafts but to provide hard-pressed working-class people with an income, from basketry and quilts in rural schools or lace-making in urban settlement houses. It's possible that Hall's story about "Aunt Jane's Album," the story from *Aunt Jane of Kentucky* that is presented in this book, was motivated by the same compassionate propaganda impulse that produced

"Sally Ann's Experience." That is, Hall wanted to put a human face on the quiltmaking tradition and unobtrusively promote it at the same time. Certainly both stories have served their writer's purposes well, one illustrating the grass roots frustrations of inequality for women, and the other praising and describing the needlework tradition among American women.

Hall, who died in 1935, wrote many more books after Aunt Jane including *The Land of Long Ago* (1909); *To Love and to Cherish* (1911); her last novel, *Clover and Bluegrass* (1916), which included her final Aunt Jane story; and a collection of poetry, *The Unspoken Word* (1931). In 1912 Hall published *A Book of Hand-Woven Coverlets,* her only nonfiction work and an interesting investigation into the history and lore of woven coverlets.

In returning Aunt Jane to the American public, Chronicle Books is bringing back to life one of our most winning and positive mythic folk heroines—the pioneer wife who stood shoulder to shoulder with her husband, raising a family, creating a community, and leaving her mark. As Aunt Jane says, quoting her Bible, most of her hard life's work "perishes with the usin'. . .but when one o' my grandchildren or great-grandchildren sees one o' these quilts, they'll think about Aunt Jane, and, wherever I am then, I'll know I ain't forgotten."

Roderick Kiracofe
SAN FRANCISCO

They were a bizarre mass of color on the sweet spring landscape, those patchwork quilts, swaying in a long line under the elms and maples. The old orchard made a blossoming background for them, and farther off on the horizon rose the beauty of fresh verdure and purple mist on those low hills, or "knobs," that are to the heart of the Kentuckian as the Alps to the Swiss or the sea to the sailor.

I opened the gate softly and paused for a moment between the blossoming lilacs that grew on each side of the path. The fragrance of the white and the purple blooms was like a resurrection-call over the graves of many a dead spring; and as I stood, shaken with thoughts as the flowers are with the winds, Aunt Jane came around from the back of the house, her black silk cape fluttering from her shoulders, and a calico sunbonnet hiding her features in its cavernous depth. She walked briskly to the clothes-line and began patting and smoothing the quilts where the breeze had disarranged them.

"Aunt Jane," I called out, "are you having a fair all by yourself?"

She turned quickly, pushing back the sunbonnet from her eyes.

"Why, child," she said with a happy laugh, "you come pretty nigh scaring me. No, I ain't having any fair; I'm just giving my quilts their spring airing. Twice a year I put them out in the sun and wind; and this morning the air smelled so sweet, I thought it was a good chance to freshen them up for the summer. It's about time to take them in now."

She began to fold the quilts and lay them over her arm, and I did the same. Back and forth we went from the clothes-line to the house, and from the house to the clothes-line, until the quilts were safely housed from the coming dewfall and piled on every available chair in the front room. I looked at them in sheer amazement. There seemed to be every pattern that the ingenuity of woman could devise and the industry of woman put together — "four-patches," "nine-patches," "log-cabins," "wild-goose chases," "rising suns," hex-agons, diamonds, and only Aunt Jane knows what else. As for color, who wouldn't have danced with joy at the sight of those reds, purples, yellows, and greens.

"Did you really make all these quilts, Aunt Jane?" I asked wonderingly.

Aunt Jane's eyes sparkled with pride.

Log-cabin Quilt "Every stitch of them, child," she said, "except the quilting. The neighbors used to come in and help some with that.

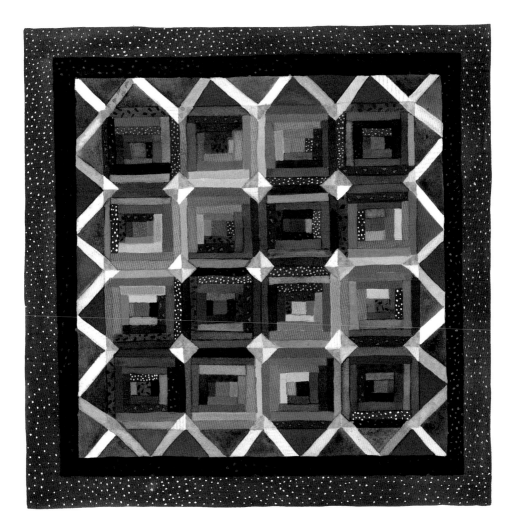

"I've heard folks say that piecing quilts was nothing but a waste of time, but that ain't always so. They used to say that Sarah Jane Mitchell would sit down right after breakfast and piece till it was time to get dinner, and then sit and piece till she had to get supper, and then piece by candlelight till she fell asleep in her chair.

"I recollect going over there one day, and Sarah Jane was getting dinner in a big hurry, for Sam had to go to town with some cattle, and there was a big basket of quilt pieces in the middle of the kitchen floor, and the house looking like a pigpen, and the children running around half naked. And Sam he laughed, and said, 'Aunt Jane, if we could wear quilts and eat quilts we'd be the richest people in the country.' Sam was the best-natured man that ever was, or he couldn't have put up with Sarah Jane's shiftless ways. Hannah Crawford said she sent Sarah Jane a bundle of calico once with Sam, and Sam always declared he lost it. But Uncle Jim Matthews said he was riding along the road just behind Sam,

Nine-patch Quilt

and he saw Sam throw it into the creek just as he got on the bridge. I never blamed Sam a bit if he did.

"But there was never any time wasted on my quilts, child. I can look at every one of them with a clear conscience. I did my work faithful; and then, when I might have set and held my hands, I'd make a block or two of patchwork, and before long I'd have enough to put together in a quilt. I went to piecing as soon as I was old enough to hold a needle and a piece of cloth, and one of the first things I can remember was sitting on the back door-step sewing my quilt pieces, and mother praising my stitches. Nowadays folks don't have to sew unless they want to, but when I was a child there weren't any sewing machines, and it was about as needful for folks to know how to sew as it was for them to know how to eat; and every child that was well raised could hem and run and backstitch and gather and overhand by the time she was nine years old. Why, I'd pieced four quilts by the time I was nineteen years old, and when Abram and I set up housekeeping I had bedclothes enough for three beds.

"I've had a heap of comfort all my life making quilts, and now in my old age I wouldn't take a fortune for them. Sit down here, child, where you can see out of the window

and smell the lilacs, and we'll look at them all. You see, some folks have albums to put folks' pictures in to remember them by, and some folks have a book to write down the things that happen every day so they won't forget them; but, honey, these quilts are my albums and my diaries, and whenever the weather's bad and I can't get out to see folks, I just spread out my quilts and look at them and study over them, and it's just like going back fifty or sixty years and living my life over again.

"There ain't nothing like a piece of calico for bringing back old times, child, unless it's a flower or a bunch of thyme or a piece of pennyroyal—anything that smells sweet. Why, I can go out yonder in the yard and gather a bunch of that purple lilac and just shut my eyes and see faces I ain't seen for fifty years, and something goes through me like a flash of lightning, and it seems like I'm young again just for that minute."

Aunt Jane's hands were stroking lovingly a "nine-patch" that resembled the coat of many colors.

"Now this quilt, honey," she said, "I made out of the pieces of my children's clothes, their little dresses and waists and aprons. Some of them's dead, and some of them's grown and married and a long way off from me, further off than the ones that's dead, I sometimes think. But when I sit down and look at this quilt and think over the pieces, it seems like they all come back, and I can see them playing around the floors and going in and out, and hear them crying and laughing and calling me just like they used to do before they grew up to men and women, and before there were any little graves of mine out in the old burying ground over there."

Wonderful imagination of motherhood that can bring childhood back from the dust of the grave and banish the wrinkles and gray hairs of age with no other talisman than a scrap of faded calico!

The old woman's hands were moving tremulously over the surface of the quilt as if they touched the golden curls of the little dream children who had vanished from her hearth so many years ago. But there were no tears either in her eyes or in her voice. I had long noticed that Aunt Jane always smiled when she spoke of the people whom the world calls "dead," or the things it calls "lost" or "past." These words seemed to have for her higher and more tender meanings than are placed on them by the sorrowful heart of humanity.

But the moments were passing, and one could not dwell too long on any quilt, however well beloved. Aunt Jane rose briskly, folded up the one that lay across her knees, and whisked out another from the huge pile on an old splint-bottomed chair.

"Here's a piece of one of Sally Ann's purple calico dresses.

Sally Ann always thought a heap of purple calico. Here's one of Milly Amos' ginghams—that pink-and-white one.

"And that piece of white with the rosebuds in it, that's Miss Penelope's. She gave it to me the summer before she died. Bless her soul! That dress just matched her face exactly. Somehow her and her clothes always looked alike, and her voice matched her face, too. One of the things I'm looking forward to, child, is seeing Miss Penelope again and hearing her sing. Voices and faces are alike; there's some that you can't remember, and there's some you can't forget. I've seen a heap of people and heard a heap of voices, but Miss Penelope's face was different from all the rest, and so was her voice. Why, if she said 'Good morning' to you, you'd hear that 'Good morning' all day, and her singing—I know there never was anything like it in the world. My grandchildren all laugh at me for thinking so much of Miss Penelope's singing, but then they never heard her, and I have: that's the difference. My grandchild Henrietta was down here three or four years ago, and she said, 'Grandma,

Path through the Woods

don't you want to go up to Louisville with me and hear Patty sing?' And I said, 'Patty who, child?' I said, 'If it was to hear Miss Penelope sing, I'd carry these old bones of mine clear from here to New York. But there ain't anybody else I want to hear sing bad enough to go up to Louisville or anywhere else. And some of these days,' I said, *'I'm going to hear Miss Penelope sing.'*"

Aunt Jane laughed blithely, and it was impossible not to laugh with her.

"Honey," she said, in the next breath, lowering her voice and laying her finger on the rosebud piece, "honey, there's one thing I can't get over. Here's a piece of Miss Penelope's dress, but *where's Miss Penelope?* Ain't it strange that a piece of calico will outlast you and me? Don't it seem like folks ought to hold on to their bodies as long as other folks hold on to a piece of the dresses they used to wear?"

Questions as old as the human heart and its human grief! An eerie feeling came over me as I entered into the old woman's mood and thought of the strong, vital bodies that had clothed themselves in those fabrics of purple and pink and white, and that now were dust and ashes lying in sad, neglected graves on farm and lonely roadside. There lay the quilt on our knees, and the gay scraps of calico seemed to mock us with their vivid colors.

Aunt Jane's cheerful voice called me back. "Here's a piece of one of my dresses," she said; "brown ground with a red ring in it. Abram picked it out. And here's another one, that light yellow ground with the vine running through it. I never had so many calico dresses that I didn't want one more, for in my day folks used to think a calico dress was good enough to wear anywhere. Abram knew my failing, and two or three times a year he'd bring me a dress when he came from town.

And the dresses he'd pick out always suited me better than the ones I picked.

"I recollect I finished this quilt the summer before Mary Frances was born, and Sally Ann and Milly Amos and Maria Petty came over and gave me a lift on the quilting. Here's Milly's work, here's Sally Ann's, and here's Maria's."

I looked, but my inexperienced eye could see no difference in the handiwork of the three women. Aunt Jane saw my look of incredulity.

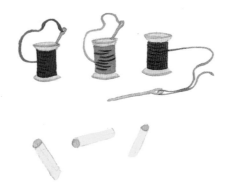

"Now, child," she said, earnestly, "you think I'm fooling you, but there's just as much difference in folks' sewing as there is in their handwriting. Milly made a fine stitch, but she couldn't keep on the line to save her life; Maria never could make a regular stitch, some would be long and some would be short, and Sally Ann's was regular, but all of them coarse. I can see them now stooping over the quilting frames—Milly talking as hard as she sewed, Sally Ann throwing in a word now and then, and Maria never opening her mouth except to ask for the thread or the chalk. I recollect they came over after dinner, and we got the quilt out of the frames long before sundown, and the next day I began binding it, and I got the premium on it that year at the Fair.

"I hardly ever showed a quilt at the Fair that I didn't take the premium, but here's one quilt that Sarah Jane Mitchell beat me on."

And Aunt Jane dragged out a ponderous, red-lined affair,

the very antithesis of the silken, down-filled comforter that rests so lightly on the couch of a modern woman.

"It makes me laugh just to think of that time, and how happy Sarah Jane was. It was way back in the fifties. I recollect we had a mighty fine Fair that year. The crops were all fine that season, and such apples and pears and grapes you never did see. The Floral Hall was full of things, and the whole county turned out to go to the Fair.

"Abram and I got there the first day bright and early, and we were walking around the amphitheater and looking at the townfolks and the sights, and we met Sally Ann. She stopped us, and said, 'Sarah Jane Mitchell's got a quilt in the Floral Hall in competition with yours and Milly Amos'.' I said, 'Is that all the competition there is?' And Sally Ann said, 'All that amounts to anything. There's one more, but it's about as bad a piece of sewing as Sarah Jane's and that looks like it would hardly hold together till the Fair's over. And,' she said, 'I don't believe there'll be any more. It looks

Schoolhouse Quilt

like this was an off year on that particular kind of quilt. I didn't get mine done,' she said, 'and neither did Marie Petty, and maybe it's a good thing after all.'

"Well I saw in a minute what Sally Ann was aiming at. And I said to Abram, 'Abram, haven't you got something to do with appointing the judges for the women's things?' And he said, 'Yes.' And I said, 'Well, you see to it that Sally Ann gets appointed to help judge the calico quilts.' And bless your soul, Abram got me and Sally Ann both appointed. The other judge was Mis' Doctor Brigham, one of the town ladies. We told her all about what we wanted to do, and she just laughed and said, 'Well, if that ain't the kindest, nicest thing! Of course we'll do it.'

"Seeing that I had a quilt there, I hadn't a bit of business being a judge; but the first thing I did was to fold my quilt up and hide it under Maria Petty's big worsted quilt, and then we pinned the blue ribbon on Sarah Jane's and the red on Milly's. I'd fixed it all up with Milly, and she was just as willing as I was for Sarah Jane to have the premium. There was just one thing I was afraid of: Milly was a good-hearted woman, but she never had much control over her tongue. And I said to her, 'Milly, it's mighty good of you to give up your chance for the premium, but if Sarah Jane ever finds out, that'll spoil everything. For,' I said, 'there ain't any kindness in doing a person a favor and then telling everybody about it.' And Milly laughed, and she said, 'I know

what you mean, Aunt Jane. It's mighty hard for me to keep from telling everything I know and some things I don't know, but,' she said, 'I'm never going to tell this, even to Sam.' And she kept her word, too. Every once in a while she'd come up to me and whisper, 'I ain't told it yet, Aunt Jane,' just to see me laugh.

Susan McPhee
1896

"As soon as the doors were open, after we'd all got through judging and putting on the ribbons, Milly went and hunted Sarah Jane up and told her that her quilt had the blue ribbon. They said the poor thing almost fainted for joy. She turned right white, and had to lean up against the post for a while before she could get to the Floral Hall. I never shall forget her face. It was worth a dozen premiums to me, and Milly, too. She just stood looking at that quilt and the blue ribbon on it, and her eyes were full of tears and her lips quivering, and then she started off and brought the children in to look at 'Mammy's quilt.' She met Sam on the way out, and she said: 'Sam, what do you reckon? My quilt took the premium.' And I believe in my soul Sam was as much pleased as Sarah Jane. He came sauntering up, trying to look unconcerned, but anybody could see he was mighty well satisfied. It does a husband and a wife a heap of good to be proud of each other, and I reckon that was the first time Sam ever had cause to be proud of poor Sarah

Album Patch Quilt

Jane. It's my belief that he thought more of Sarah Jane all the rest of her life just on account of that premium. Me and Sally Ann helped her pick it out. She had her choice between a butterdish and a cup, and she took the cup.

"Folks used to laugh and say that that cup was the only thing in Sarah Jane's house that was kept clean and bright, and if it hadn't been solid silver, she'd have worn it all out rubbing it up. Sarah Jane died of pneumonia about three or four years after that, and the folks that nursed her said she wouldn't take a drink of water or a dose of medicine out of any cup but that. There's some folks, child, that don't have to do anything but walk along and hold out their hands, and the premiums just naturally fall into them; and there's others that work and strive the best they know how, and nothing ever seems to come to them; and I reckon nobody but the Lord and Sarah Jane knows how much happiness she got out of that cup. I'm thankful she had that much pleasure before she died."

There was a quilt hanging over the foot of the bed that had about it a certain air of distinction. It was a solid mass of patchwork, composed of squares, parallelograms, and hexagons. The squares were dark gray and red-brown, the hexagons were white, the parallelograms black and light gray. I felt sure that it had a history that set it apart from its ordinary fellows.

"Where did you get the pattern, Aunt Jane?" I asked. "I never saw anything like it."

The old lady's eyes sparkled, and she laughed with pure pleasure.

"That's what everybody says," she exclaimed, jumping up and spreading the favored quilt over two laden chairs, where its merits became more apparent and striking. "There ain't another quilt like this in the State of Kentucky, or the world, for that matter. My granddaughter Henrietta, Mary Frances' youngest child, brought me this pattern *from Europe.*"

She spoke the words as one might say, "from Paradise," or "from Olympus," or "from the Lost Atlantis." "Europe" was evidently a name to conjure with, a country of mystery and romance unspeakable. I had seen many things from many lands beyond the sea, but a quilt pattern from Europe! Here at last was something new under the sun. In what shop of London or Paris were quilt patterns kept on sale for the American tourist?

"You see," said Aunt Jane, "Henrietta married a mighty rich man, and just as good as he's rich, too, and they went to Europe on their honeymoon. When she came home she brought me the prettiest shawl you ever saw. She made me stand up and shut my eyes, and she put it on my shoulders and made me look in the looking-glass, and then she said, 'I brought you a new quilt pattern, too, grandma, and I want you to piece one quilt by it and leave it to me when you die.' And then she told me about going to a town they call Florence, and how she went into a big church that was built *Mosaic Quilt*

hundreds of years before I was born. And she said the floor was made of little pieces of colored stone, all laid together in a pattern, and they called it mosaic. And I said, 'Honey, has it got anything to do with Moses and his law?' You know the Commandments was called the Mosaic Law, and was all on tables of stone. And Henrietta just laughed, and said: 'No, Grandma; I don't believe it has. But,' she said, 'the minute I stepped on that pavement I thought about you, and I drew this pattern on a piece of paper and brought it all the way to Kentucky for you to make a quilt by.' Henrietta bought the worsted for me, for she said it had to be just the colors of that pavement, and I made it that very winter."

Aunt Jane was regarding the quilt with worshipful eyes.

"Many a time while I was piecing that," she said, "I thought about the man that laid the pavement in that old church, and wondered what his name was, and how he looked, and what he'd think if he knew there was a old woman down here in Kentucky using his patterns to make a bedquilt."

It was indeed a far cry from the Florentine artisan of centuries ago to this humble worker in calico and worsted, but between the two stretched a cord of sympathy that made them one—the eternal aspiration after beauty.

"Honey," Aunt Jane said, suddenly, "did I ever show you my premiums?"

And then, with pleasant excitement in her manner, she arose, fumbled in her deep pocket for an ancient bunch of keys, and unlocked a cupboard on one side of the fireplace. One by one she drew them out, unrolled the soft yellow tissue-paper that enfolded them, and ranged them in a stately line on the old cherry center-table; nineteen sterling silver cups and goblets. "Abram took some of them on his fine stock, and I took some of them on my quilts and salt-rising bread and cakes," she said impressively.

To the artist his medals, to the soldier his cross of the Legion of Honor, and to Aunt Jane her silver cups! All the triumph of a humble life was symbolized in these shining things. They were simple and genuine as the days in which they were made. A few of them boasted a beaded edge or a golden lining, but no engraving or embossing marred their silver purity. On the bottom of each was the stamp: "John B. Akin, Danville, Ky." There they stood, filled to the brim with precious memories of the times when she and Abram had worked together in field or garden or home, and the County Fair brought to all a yearly opportunity to stand on the height of achievement and know somewhat the taste of Fame's enchanted cup.

"There's one for every child and grandchild," she said, quietly, as she began wrapping them in the silky paper, and storing them carefully away in the cupboard, there to rest until the day when children and grandchildren would claim them to stand as heirlooms on fashionable sideboards and damask-covered tables.

"Did you ever think, child," she said, presently, "how much piecing a quilt's like living a life? And as for sermons, why, there's no better sermon to me than a patchwork quilt, and the doctrines are right there a lot plainer then they are in the catechism. Many a time I've sat and listened to Parson Page preaching about predestination and free will, and I've said to myself, 'Well, I ain't never been through Center College up at Danville, but if I could just get up in the pulpit with one of my quilts, I could make it a heap plainer to folks than parson's making it with all his big words.'

"You see, you start out with just so much calico; you don't go to the store and pick it out and buy it, but the neighbors will give you a piece here and a piece there, and you'll have a piece every time you cut out a dress, and you take just what happens to come. And that's like predestination. But when it comes to the cutting out, why, you're free to choose your own pattern. You can give the same kind of pieces to two persons, and one'll make a 'nine-patch' and one'll make a 'wild-goose chase,' and there'll be two quilts made out of the same kind of pieces, and just as different as they can be. And that is just the way with the living. The

Lord sends us the pieces, but we can cut them out and put them together pretty much to suit ourselves, and there's a heap more in the cutting out and the sewing than there is in the calico. The same sort of things comes into all lives, just as the Apostle says, 'There hath no trouble taken you but is common to all men.'

"The same trouble'll come into two people's lives, and one'll take it and make one thing out of it, and the other'll make something entirely different. There was Mary Harris and Mandy Crawford. They both lost their husbands the same year; and Mandy sat down and cried and worried and wondered what on earth she was going to do, and the farm went to wrack and the children turned out bad, and she had to live with her son-in-law in her old age. But Mary, she got up and went to work, and made everybody about her work, too; and she managed the farm better than it ever had been managed before, and the boys all came up steady, hardworking men, and there wasn't a woman in the county better fixed up than Mary Harris. Things are predestined to come to us, honey, but we're just as free as air to make what we please out of them. And when it comes to putting the pieces together, there's another time when we're free. You don't trust to luck for the calico to put your quilt together with; you go to the store and pick it out yourself, any color you like.

"There's folks that always look on the bright side and make the best of everything, and that's like putting your quilt together with blue or pink or white or some other pretty color; and there's folks that never see anything

but the dark side, and always looking for trouble, and treasuring it up after they get it, and they're putting their lives together with some dark, ugly color. You can spoil the prettiest quilt pieces that ever was made just by putting them together with black, just like you would put a quilt together with the wrong color, and the best sort of life is miserable if you don't look at things right and think about them right.

"Then there's another thing. I've seen folks piece and piece, but when it comes to putting the blocks together and quilting and lining it, they'd give it out; and that's like folks that do a little here and a little there, but their lives ain't of much use after all, any more than a lot of loose pieces of patchwork. And then while you're living your life, it looks pretty much like a jumble of quilt pieces before they're put together; but when you get through with it, or pretty nigh through, as I am now, you'll see the use and the purpose of everything in it. Everything'll be in its right place just like the squares in this 'four-patch,' and one piece may be pretty

and another one ugly, but it all looks right when you see it finished and joined together."

Did I say that every pattern was represented? No, there was one notable omission. Not a single "crazy quilt" was there in the collection. I called Aunt Jane's attention to this lack.

"Child," she said, "I used to say there wasn't anything I couldn't do if I made up my mind to it. But I hadn't seen a 'crazy quilt' then. The first one I ever saw was up at Danville at Mary Frances', and Henrietta said, 'Now, Grandma, you've got to make a crazy quilt; you've made every other sort that ever was heard of.' And she brought me the pieces and showed me how to base them on the square, and she said she'd work the fancy stitches around them for me. Well, I sat there all the morning trying to fix up that square, and the *Crazy Quilt* more I tried, the uglier and crookeder the thing looked. And

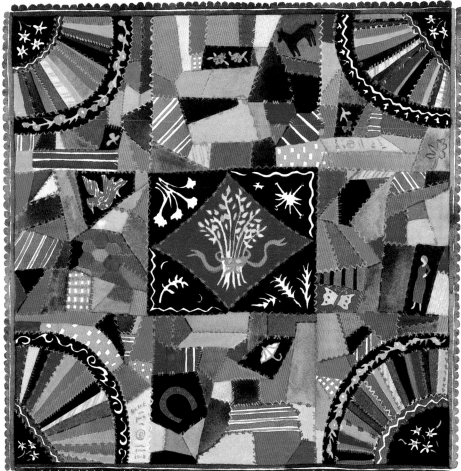

finally I said: 'Here, child, take your pieces. If I was to make this the way you want me to, there'd be a crazy quilt and a crazy woman, too.'"

Aunt Jane was laying the folded quilts in neat piles here and there about the room. There was a look of unspeakable satisfaction on her face—the look of the creator who sees the work completed and pronounces it good.

"I've been a hard worker all my life," she said, seating herself and folding her hands restfully, "but 'most all my work has been the kind that perishes with the using,' as the Bible says. That's the discouraging thing about a woman's work. Milly Amos used to say that if a woman was to see all the dishes that she had to wash before she died, piled up before her in one pile, she'd lie down and die right then and there. I've always had the name of being a good house-keeper, but when I'm dead and gone there ain't anybody going to think of the floors I've swept, and the tables I've scrubbed, and the old clothes I've patched, and the stockings

I've darned. But when one of my grandchildren or great-grandchildren sees one of these quilts, they'll think about Aunt Jane, and, wherever I am then, I'll know I ain't forgotten.

"I reckon everybody wants to leave something behind that'll last after they're dead and gone. It don't look like it's worthwhile to live unless you can do that. The Bible says folks 'rest from their labors, and their works do follow them,' but that ain't so. They go, and maybe they do rest, but their works stay right here, unless they're the sort that don't outlast the using. Now, some folks have money to build monuments with—great, tall, marble pillars, with angels on top of them, like you see in Cave Hill and them big city burying grounds. And some folks can build churches and schools and hospitals to keep folks in mind of them, but all the work I've got to leave behind me is just these quilts, and sometimes, when I'm sitting here, working with my calico and gingham pieces, I'll finish off a block, and

laugh and say to myself, 'Well, here's another stone for the monument.'

"I reckon you think, child, that a calico or a worsted quilt is a curious sort of a monument—about as perishable as the sweeping and scrubbing and mending. But if folks value things rightly, and know how to take care of them, there ain't many things that'll last longer than a quilt. Why, I've got a blue and white counterpane that mother's mother spun and wove, and there ain't a sign of giving out in it yet. I'm going to will that to my grandaughter that lives in Danville, Mary Frances' oldest child. She was down here last summer, and I was looking over my things and packing them away, and she happened to see that counterpane, and she said, 'Grandma, I want you to will me that.' And I said: 'What do you want with that old thing, honey? You know you wouldn't sleep under such a counterpane as that.' And she said, 'No, but I'd hang it up over my parlor door for a . . .'"

Blue-and-White Counterpane

"Portiere?" I suggested, as Aunt Jane hesitated for the unaccustomed word.

"That's it, child. Somehow I can't recollect these newfangled words, any more than I can understand these newfangled ways. Who'd ever have thought that folks would go to stringing up bed-coverings in their doors? And I said to Janie, 'You can hang your great-great-grandmother's counterpane up in your parlor door if you want to, but,' I said, 'don't you ever make a door-curtain out of one of my quilts.' The way things turn around, if I was to come back fifty years from now, like as not I'd find them using my quilts for window curtains or door-mats."

We both laughed, and there rose in my mind a picture of a twentieth-century house decorated with Aunt Jane's "nine-patches" and "rising suns." How could the dear old woman know that the same aesthetic sense that had drawn *Rising Sun Quilt* from their obscurity the white and blue counterpanes of

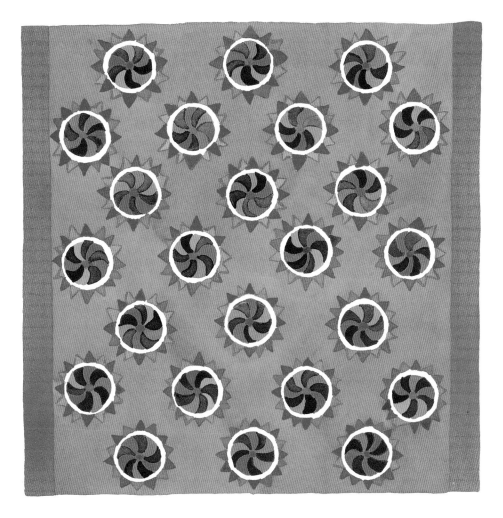

colonial days would forever protect her loved quilts from such a desecration as she feared?

As she lifted a pair of quilts from a chair nearby, I caught sight of a pure white spread in striking contrast with the many-hued patchworks.

"Where did you get that Marseilles spread, Aunt Jane?" I asked, pointing to it. Aunt Jane lifted it and laid it on my lap without a word. Evidently she thought that here was something that could speak for itself. It was two layers of snowy cotton cloth thinly lined with cotton, and elaborately quilted into a perfect imitation of a Marseilles counterpane. The pattern was a tracery of roses, buds, and leaves, very much conventionalized, but still recognizable for the things they were. The stitches were fairylike, and altogether it might have covered the bed of a queen.

"I made every stitch of that spread the year before Abram and I were married," she said. "I put it on my bed when we went to housekeeping; it was on the bed when

Abram died, and when I die I want them to cover me with it." There was a life-history in the simple words. I thought of Desdemona and her bridal sheets, and I did not offer to help Aunt Jane as she folded this quilt.

"I reckon you think," she resumed presently, "that I'm a mean, stingy old creature not to give Janie the counterpane now, instead of hoarding it up, and all these quilts too, and keeping folks waiting for them till I die. But, honey, it ain't all selfishness. I'd give away my best dress or my best bonnet or an acre of ground to anybody that needed them more than I did; but these quilts—why, it looks like my whole life was sewed up in them and I ain't going to part with them while life lasts."

There was a ring of passionate eagerness in the old voice, and she fell to putting away her treasures as if the suggestion of losing them had made her fearful of their safety.

I looked again at the heap of quilts. An hour ago they had been patchwork, and nothing more. But now! The old woman's words had wrought a transformation in the homely mass of calico and silk and worsted. Patchwork? Ah, no! It was memory, imagination, history, biography, joy, sorrow, philosophy, religion, romance, realism, life, love, and death; and over all, like a halo, the love of the artist for her work and soul's longing for earthly immortality.

No wonder the wrinkled fingers smoothed them as reverently as we handle the garments of the dead.

Anna Price-Oneglia is a Monterey Bay–area painter. She was born in New York City and studied at the Cooper Union School of Art and the Boston Museum School of Fine Art.

Her primary medium is watercolor, as are the illustrations in this book, but lately she is working in mixed media and lithography, as well. Her work is available on cards from Marcel Schurman Co. and Pomegranate Publications. She hopes to illustrate a children's book next.

Bar Quilt